Day at the Fair

For my brother, Mike—P. H.

To Ellen—K. M.

LITTLE SIMON
An imprint of Simon & Schuster Children's Publishing Division
1230 Avenue of the Americas
New York, New York 10020
Text and illustrations copyright © 2000 by Simon & Schuster, Inc.
The names and depictions of Raggedy Ann and Raggedy Andy are trademarks of Simon & Schuster.
READY-TO-READ, LITTLE SIMON, and colophon are registered trademarks of Simon & Schuster.
Manufactured in the United States of America
First Edition
2 4 6 8 10 9 7 5 3 1

Library of Congress Cataloging-in-Publication Data
Hall, Patricia, 1948-
Day at the fair / by Patricia Hall ; illustrated by Kathryn Mitter.
p. cm. — (Classic Raggedy Ann & Andy) (Ready-to-read)
Summary: While Marcella is at the fair, Raggedy Ann and the other dolls create a fair of their own in
her room and almost get into trouble.
ISBN 0-689-83248-6
[1. Dolls—Fiction. 2. Fairs—Fiction.] I. Mitter, Kathy, ill. II. Title. III. Series. IV. Series: Ready-to-read
PZ7.H147515 Rae 2000
[E]-dc21   99-056167

Day at the Fair

by Patricia Hall
illustrated by Kathryn Mitter

Ready-to-Read

Little Simon

New York   London   Toronto   Sydney   Singapore

"I can't wait until tomorrow comes!" Marcella told
Raggedy Ann and Andy. "I'm going to the fair! I'm
sorry I can't take you. But you might get lost."

The Raggedys didn't say a word. Everyone
knows that rag dolls can't talk. At least that's what
Marcella thought.

Later, after Marcella had gone to bed, Raggedy
Andy sat up. "Why can't we go with Marcella?" he
asked.

"Because fairs aren't for dolls, they're for people,"

said Raggedy Ann. "But, I'll tell you what! Tomorrow we'll make our own fair right here!"

Raggedy Andy was so excited, he could hardly sleep.

 7

The next morning Marcella kissed her dolls good-bye and hugged Fido.

"I'll be back when the clock says 'cuckoo' two times," she said. "Be good children!"

Click went the front door. Marcella and Daddy were gone.

Slam went the back door. Mama went outside to her garden.

"Finally!" said Raggedy Andy.

"Let the fair begin!" said Raggedy Ann, giggling.

"Up I go!" cried Raggedy Ann.

"This is our very own bouncing place!" said Uncle Clem.

"Look out below!" shouted Raggedy Andy.

"Step right up! Three balls for a wooden nickel," called Raggedy Ann.

"Great shot!" said the Camel with the Wrinkled Knees.

"Uncle Clem gets a prize!" said Raggedy Andy.

"Now let's slide," said Raggedy Ann.

Uncle Clem went first.

"Whee!" he cried on the way down. "Who says fairs aren't for dolls!"

"Me next!" said Raggedy Andy.

"Be careful!" cried Raggedy Ann.

But out the window went Raggedy Andy—
heading straight for Mama's tulips!

Uncle Clem reached down to help.

"Hold on," cried the Camel with the Wrinkled
Knees.

But Uncle Clem went sailing toward Mama's
favorite rosebush. Now there were two dolls
outside!

The Camel with the Wrinkled Knees reached down to help.

"Watch out!" cried Fido. But down went the Camel. Now there were three dolls outside!

"Fido," said Raggedy Ann. "Follow me to the basement. We're on a rescue mission!"

Raggedy Ann sat down on the basement floor and thought so hard that she nearly burst three stitches in her rag-doll head.

Then she said to Fido, "Quick, out that window! You help Uncle Clem and Camel. I'll help Raggedy Andy."

"Pssst! Over here!" said Raggedy Ann to Raggedy
Andy. She didn't want Mama to hear.

"I'm coming!" said Raggedy Andy. He didn't want
Mama to see.

"Grab on!" Fido said, holding his paw out to Uncle Clem.

"Hold tight!" Fido said to the Camel with the Wrinkled Knees, pulling as hard as he could.

"Way to go, Fido!" Raggedy Andy cheered.

"I knew you could do it!" said Raggedy Ann. "Now it's time to get back upstairs before Mama comes inside."

"Hurry!" whispered Raggedy Ann.

"Fido, is that you?" called Mama from the kitchen.

"Arf!" barked Fido.

"I didn't know fairs were this exciting!" said Raggedy Andy. "But it's lucky we're rag dolls. Falling didn't hurt a bit!"

"Speak for yourself!" said Uncle Clem, laughing.

"It's time to clean ourselves up," said Raggedy Ann.

"One more knee to clean," said Uncle Clem.

"Hold still!" said Raggedy Ann.

"Good as new," said the Camel with the
Wrinkled Knees.

25

"Now let's clean up this room!" said Raggedy Ann.

"Aw, gee," said the Camel with the Wrinkled
Knees. "Can't we play more at the fair?"

"No, we'd better get moving," said Raggedy
Andy when he saw the look on his sister's face.

27

Before long the playroom was as good as new.
Then the dolls and Fido heard "cuckoo! cuckoo!"

And everyone remembered—two cuckoos meant
Marcella would be home soon!

Marcella came in a few minutes later.

"I've missed you!" she said to the dolls and Fido.
"But I know you've been good. Look! I brought
surprises!"

Then Marcella told the dolls and Fido all about
her day at the fair.

"First I jumped on a bouncy trampoline,"
Marcella said. "Then I threw some balls and won a
prize. Then I slid down a high-up slippery-slide. I
was careful not to fall off."

Then Marcella stopped and looked at her dolls. "Oh," she said. "I guess you wouldn't understand. Fairs are for people, not dolls."

Raggedy Ann and Andy and Uncle Clem and the Camel with the Wrinkled Knees sat very still. None of them said a word.

Because, of course, everyone knows rag dolls can't talk!